A Note to Parents and Caregivers:

Read-it! Readers are for children who are just starting on the amazing road to reading. These beautiful books support both the acquisition of reading skills and the love of books.

The RED LEVEL presents familiar topics using common words and repeating sentence patterns.

The BLUE LEVEL presents new ideas using a larger vocabulary and varied sentence structure.

The YELLOW LEVEL presents more challenging ideas, a broad vocabulary, and wide variety in sentence structure.

When sharing a book with your child, read in short stretches, pausing often to talk about the pictures. Have your child turn the pages and point to the pictures and familiar words. And be sure to reread favorite stories or parts of stories.

There is no right or wrong way to share books with children. Find time to read with your child and pass on the legacy of literacy.

Adria F. Klein, Ph.D.
Professor Emeritus
California State University
San Bernardino, California

First American edition published in 2003 by
Picture Window Books
5115 Excelsior Boulevard
Suite 232
Minneapolis, MN 55416
1-877-845-8392
www.picturewindowbooks.com

First published in Great Britain by Franklin Watts, 96 Leonard Street, London, EC2A 4XD
Text © Anne Cassidy 2000
Illustration © Colin Paine 2000

Printed in the United States of America.
1 2 3 4 5 6 08 07 06 05 04 03

Library of Congress Cataloging-in-Publication Data
Cassidy, Anne.
  The crying princess / written by Anne Cassidy ; illustrated by Colin Paine.
    p. cm. — (Read-it! readers)
  Summary: No one can stop Princess Alice from crying, until Prince Tom arrives with a good solution.
  ISBN 1-4048-0053-0
  [1. Crying—Fiction. 2. Princesses—Fiction. 3. Kings, queens, rulers, etc.—Fiction. 4. Princes—Fiction.) I. Paine, Colin, ill. II. Title. III. Series.
  PZ7.26854 Cr 2003
  [E]—dc21   2002072296

PICTURE WINDOW BOOKS

The Crying
Princess

Written by Anne Cassidy

Illustrated by Colin Paine

Reading Advisors:
Adria F. Klein, Ph.D.
Professor Emeritus, California State University
San Bernardino, California

Ruth Thomas
Durham Public Schools
Durham, North Carolina

R. Ernice Bookout
Durham Public Schools
Durham, North Carolina

Picture Window Books
Minneapolis, Minnesota

Princess Alice cried
all the time.

She howled in the morning.
She sobbed in the afternoon.

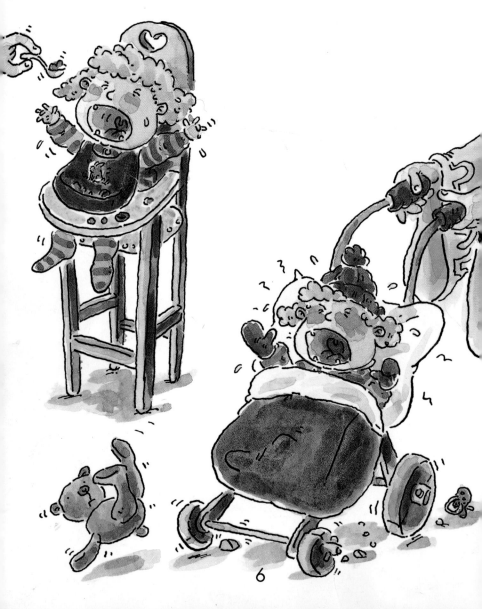

The queen was not happy.
She put cotton in her ears.

The king gave Alice a crown and some sparkling jewels.

Princess Alice cried harder.

The jester tried to help.
He told a funny joke.

Princess Alice screamed
even louder.

The wizard cast a spell.

Princess Alice snapped his wand in two.

The king didn't know what to do.

"I'll give all my gold to anyone who can make her stop crying," he said.

Prince Tom came from a land far, far away.

"I can make the princess stop crying," he said.

"Take off that silly crown," he told the king.

"Now, pick her up!"
he told the queen.

"Give her some milk to drink," said Prince Tom.

Princess Alice stopped
crying.

The jester and the wizard
were both very pleased.

The king gave all his gold to Prince Tom.

Everyone was full of joy—

except for the king and
queen.

They had no gold left.

The queen cried
and sobbed.

The king howled
and screamed.

So, Princess Alice put
cotton in her ears!

Red Level

The Best Snowman, by Margaret Nash 1-4048-0048-4
Bill's Baggy Pants, by Susan Gates 1-4048-0050-6
Cleo and Leo, by Anne Cassidy 1-4048-0049-2
Felix on the Move, by Maeve Friel 1-4048-0055-7
Jasper and Jess, by Anne Cassidy 1-4048-0061-1
The Lazy Scarecrow, by Jillian Powell 1-4048-0062-X
Little Joe's Big Race, by Andy Blackford 1-4048-0063-8
The Little Star, by Deborah Nash 1-4048-0065-4
The Naughty Puppy, by Jillian Powell 1-4048-0067-0
Selfish Sophie, by Damian Kelleher 1-4048-0069-7

Blue Level

The Bossy Rooster, by Margaret Nash 1-4048-0051-4
Jack's Party, by Ann Bryant 1-4048-0060-3
Little Red Riding Hood, by Maggie Moore 1-4048-0064-6
Recycled!, by Jillian Powell 1-4048-0068-9
The Sassy Monkey, by Anne Cassidy 1-4048-0058-1
The Three Little Pigs, by Maggie Moore 1-4048-0071-9

Yellow Level

Cinderella, by Barrie Wade 1-4048-0052-2
The Crying Princess, by Anne Cassidy 1-4048-0053-0
Eight Enormous Elephants, by Penny Dolan 1-4048-0054-9
Freddie's Fears, by Hilary Robinson 1-4048-0056-5
Goldilocks and the Three Bears, by Barrie Wade 1-4048-0057-3
Mary and the Fairy, by Penny Dolan 1-4048-0066-2
Jack and the Beanstalk, by Maggie Moore 1-4048-0059-X
The Three Billy Goats Gruff, by Barrie Wade 1-4048-0070-0